# FINN & BOTTS

*DOUBLE TROUBLE AT THE MUSEUM*

# FINN & BOTTS

*DOUBLE TROUBLE AT THE MUSEUM*

## STEW KNIGHT

Dreamwell Press

Copyright © 2019 Stewart Knight

Published by Dreamwell Press, Salt Lake City
www.finnandbotts.com

Edited and designed by Girl Friday Productions
www.girlfridayproductions.com

Editorial: Clete Smith, Amy Sullivan, Amy Snyder
Design: Paul Barrett
Illustrations: Mark Meyers

ISBN (Paperback): 978-1-7336092-1-0

First edition

Printed in the United States of America

*For Jake*

# CHAPTER ONE

Finn Fasser always looked forward to seeing the dinosaurs at the city museum. But he never thought he would be sleeping next to them.

"I hope T. rex is ready for me!" Finn shouted as he opened the front door. Finn had just come home after spending the entire afternoon reading the *Extraordinary Dinosaur Encyclopedia* with Botts, his best friend. They had locked themselves in Botts's room so no one would bother them—except for Botts's mom. Anyone with snacks and treats was always welcome.

"Sounds like someone's excited for the museum sleepover tonight," Finn's dad replied as he came up the basement stairs. "Just as excited as I am about my new jingle." Mr. Fasser had just finished writing a commercial tune in his music studio downstairs for an advertising client.

"Here it is," Finn said as he walked down the hallway and into the kitchen. He pulled out a white card from his school backpack. It was the official invitation to the sleepover. Finn's teacher, Ms. Twitchel, had arranged the sleepover after Finn's class won the school dinosaur contest a month ago. "Ms. Twitchel said in class today that all students need to bring this if they want to get in. I can't wait to find out about the mysterious new dinosaur. Our class will be one of the first ones to see it."

Mr. Fasser read the card out loud.

# SLEEP WITH THE DINOSAURS!

## YOU ARE INVITED TO A SLEEPOVER

## AT THE KEALSTAL CITY MUSEUM ON

# MAY 17

Please arrive at 7:00 p.m.

Enter via Museum Street (behind the museum).

Bring your own sleeping bag and gear.

We will sleep in the Dinosaur Gallery.

Dinner includes pizza and drinks.

Museum staff will be with the school group throughout the night.

We will tour the museum and make a replica of a new dinosaur fossil.

For questions, call museum staff members during business hours.

———

For each student who attends, the museum receives donations from its sponsors toward the Save the Dinosaurs fundraiser.

These donations will be used to complete the new dinosaur exhibit.

Finn glowed with excitement.

"Do you think you can sleep with a T. rex staring at you all night?" Mr. Fasser asked.

"No worries," Finn replied. "We're sleeping right behind the Triceratops. And the museum map shows the Triceratops in front of the T. rex. The T. rex won't even know we're there until we sneak up on him."

"A fundraiser to *save* dinosaurs?" Selina questioned. Selina was Finn's older sister. She came down from her room after overhearing Mr. Fasser read the invitation.

"Everyone knows dinosaurs are extinct!" she said, smiling.

"Very funny," Finn said. He glared at Selina. "A new dinosaur skeleton has been discovered and—"

"A new pile of bones," interrupted Selina. "The neighborhood dogs would love this!"

"Maybe *you* could become extinct, Selina," Finn replied.

"At least temporarily," Mr. Fasser said with a wink as he glanced at Selina. "Don't you have some homework to do?" He looked back at Finn. "After you grab your stuff for tonight, call Botts and tell him we'll pick him up in two hours."

At 6:30 p.m., Finn and his dad drove to Botts's house.

"You're going to see not only dinosaurs," Finn's dad explained, "but probably a lot of other things like ice-age mammals and even some fancy rocks. I have a feeling you'll be doing everything *but* sleeping. The museum is a big place."

Mr. Fasser reached into a compartment between the front seats of the car. He pulled out a small silver flashlight and handed it to

Finn. "Keep this with you, just in case you need it," he said.

"Thanks, Dad," Finn said. "Ms. Twitchel said there will be museum employees helping us find our way around and even some security guards, if we need them."

Botts walked down his driveway as they drove up. Mr. Fasser got out and put Botts's bags in the rear of the car, next to Finn's. Botts opened the car door and sat down next to Finn in the back.

Finn handed Botts a sack of chocolate chip cookies. "All yours," Finn said. "My mom just made them this morning."

"Now I know why I like you," Botts said, laughing. He looked inside the sack and licked his lips.

"I thought you might need something to keep you going tonight," Finn replied.

Botts grabbed four cookies and started eating. His teeth could barely be seen underneath the chewy, gooey mess drizzling out of his mouth.

As Mr. Fasser drove to the freeway entrance, Finn gazed at the tall buildings of the city center in the distance. In less than thirty minutes, he would be standing next to dinosaurs as tall as some of those buildings.

"I almost forgot," Botts blurted. "My mom said there was a news report today about dinosaur bones missing from the museum. No one has been able to find them. The museum even said that some of the missing bones are from the new exhibit. Who would want to take dino bones?"

"I don't think the museum needs to worry about someone taking dinosaur bones tonight," Mr. Fasser replied. "It would be tough to sneak anything out with you and the rest of the students inside the museum."

Finn began thinking about the size and weight of the bones he had seen in Botts's dinosaur book.

"Just think if someone tried to take an Apatosaurus femur or the skull of a Torosaurus, with its huge frill," Finn said.

"And good luck trying to carry them out the front doors," Botts added.

Finn, Botts, and Mr. Fasser all laughed.

*But what if there were someone trying to take dinosaur bones from the museum tonight?* Finn thought. He felt a cold tingling sensation race down his arms and legs.

# CHAPTER TWO

As they drove past the city museum, Finn and Botts peered through the car window at the banner on the front side announcing the new exhibit. A Velociraptor and a Tyrannosaurus rex were just two of the dinosaurs shown on the banner.

"You can't really believe a Velociraptor was smarter than a T. rex," Botts argued. "Besides, T. rex was so much bigger and stronger."

"Velociraptor was faster than T. rex and hunted in packs," Finn responded. "Size didn't matter."

Mr. Fasser turned onto a small side street that led to the museum warehouse in the rear. Two employees were waiting to greet them in the parking lot.

Mr. Fasser handed Finn and Botts their bags. "Let me know which one of you stays awake longer," Finn's dad said, smiling. "You've got a busy night. See you both tomorrow."

After waving goodbye, they followed the signs to the warehouse entrance with their bags. A line had formed outside the warehouse doors with the other students who had just arrived. Finn looked up at the high stone walls. His imagination began to wander. The museum looked like a giant fortress. He pictured guards in each corner, standing alert for intruders.

Finn glanced over at a truck parked in the loading area. The rays from the sun were now low in the sky, causing something to sparkle

and shimmer inside the truck where the driver was sitting. The driver had his head tilted back against the seat and seemed to be asleep.

But then the driver moved, and the sparkling stopped. He peered out from the window and quickly turned away. *What was sparkling?* wondered Finn. *Probably just a reflection of the light off the truck window,* he thought. Suddenly someone yelled from inside the museum warehouse. Finn and Botts entered the rear doors and stopped.

"Welcome!" the museum director shouted. She was standing in the middle of the warehouse, next to a table stacked with brochures. Her hair seemed to go in every direction. "I'm Dinah Thornton, director of the museum. Please hand your invitations to one of our staff members. After you take a museum guide from the table, you'll go through the doors in front of you and into the museum. You will then follow the arrows to the Dinosaur Gallery. Your sleeping bags can go anywhere within the roped areas. We'll be starting in fifteen minutes."

Finn and Botts did not hear a word she said. Their eyes scanned the warehouse in awe. Shelves filled with crates and boxes lined the walls from floor to ceiling. On the left side of the warehouse were some tables covered with masks and costumes, life-size stone statues, wooden musical instruments, and even some swords and spears. On the right side, the tables were filled with different types of dinosaur bones encased in plaster, along with a few animals being prepared for display. Lifelike models dressed in clothing from different cultures were standing near the front wall of the warehouse.

"If dinosaur bones were missing, you would never know it with all this stuff in here," Finn said as he looked on in amazement.

"This place is huge," Botts added.

"Strange," Director Thornton said to a nearby staff member. "Someone has moved that crate from our new exhibit." Director Thornton pointed to a steel cart near the front doors of the warehouse leading into the museum. On the cart was a big tall wood crate. It was marked with the words Fragile and Do Not Open on top and New Exhibit on the ends.

Director Thornton looked over at Finn and Botts. They were partially blocking the rear entrance as they stared at the objects in the warehouse. Both were oblivious to the rest of the students trying to push past them.

"Since you two don't seem to be in a hurry to find a place to sleep," the director said, "can you help our staff member here return a crate to the Dinosaur Gallery?"

"Hi," the staff member said. "My name is Bart." His eyes darted back and forth while he talked. "Come with me."

Finn and Botts followed Bart to the front of the warehouse. Botts grabbed Finn and pointed as they neared the doors.

"Check out those cool caveman costumes," Botts said excitedly.

"They look just as real as the raptor and T. rex costumes near that rack," Finn added. "I bet the T. rex costume is twice as tall as you."

"That T. rex is actually a remote-controlled robot," Bart interrupted. "Maybe there will be a time tonight to show you how it works. For now, go ahead and put your bags right next to the crate. You can help me guide the cart by holding on to the crate."

Finn and Botts dropped their bags on the cart and grabbed the handles. Bart pushed the cart out the doorway into the museum.

The McKinnsey twins, Manny and Danny, were right behind them. They had overheard Finn and Botts talking. Both liked to play pranks on everyone at school. They were always getting into trouble.

"I think the caveman costumes would be perfect for both of you," Manny said, giggling. "It's about time both of you become cavemen."

"A good fit for your underdeveloped brains," Danny said, laughing.

"And for those of us with highly developed brains," Manny added, "the raptor costumes over there would be a better fit."

"We should actually try those on some-time," Danny said excitedly.

As the McKinnsey twins pushed their way past Botts, he lost his balance and fell against the crate. The cart turned and banged against the doors.

"If the McKinnsey twins could walk using their eyes rather than their hands," Ms. Twitchel said loudly for all to hear, "we wouldn't have students running into doors. Move it along, you two."

Botts leaned over to Finn and laughed quietly. "If the McKinnsey twins are willing to measure their brain power with a dinosaur, I think we're safe."

Bart, Finn, and Botts pushed the cart away from the warehouse doors and into the open rotunda of the museum. Finn glanced at the signs and banners hanging from the ceiling announcing the new dinosaur exhibit. He immediately grabbed Botts and pointed.

Neither of them cared which direction they were going now. Instead, they gazed at the gigantic object in the middle. It was a terrifying sight.

# CHAPTER THREE

In the center of the rotunda was the skeleton of a towering dinosaur with long spines on its back. It had a huge crocodile-shaped skull with long razor-sharp teeth. Finn left the cart and walked over to the exhibit. He read the display sign out loud.

*Spinosaurus was fifty feet long and over eighteen feet tall at the top of its spines. It was one of the largest carnivorous dinosaurs and weighed around seven tons.*

"I think T. rex has some competition," Finn said, marveling.

"Absolutely!" Bart said. "Although they lived in different time periods, Spinosaurus was probably bigger than T. rex. In fact, a T. rex may have faced death with an attack from a Spinosaurus."

Finn redirected his gaze to the main entrance of the museum. Near the main doors, two security guards stood watching them and the other students as they walked through the rotunda. Next to the main entrance was the gift shop. And standing in front of the gift shop was the replica of a raptor, its mouth wide open, showing sharp, curved teeth. A sign hung from its neck.

---

# SAVE THE DINOSAURS

## PLEASE FEED ME

Your donations will help build our new exhibit

---

"If you haven't put your hand in a dinosaur's mouth lately, here's your chance," Bart said jokingly. "This one even talks."

Botts couldn't resist. For Botts, anything associated with eating seemed appealing. After they guided the cart over to the raptor, Botts grabbed some change from his pocket and nervously dropped it into the raptor's mouth. The raptor made a hissing scream. Botts jumped back and turned around with an embarrassed look.

"Looks like the T. rex fanatic got scared of a raptor," Finn said, laughing.

"We've got five minutes before the sleepover starts," Bart said. "Even though it's roped

off, let's go through the Minerals and Gems Gallery on the right. It's closest to us and leads right to the Dinosaur Gallery. You'll be able see the other galleries later tonight."

As the cart rolled through the gallery, Finn lost count of the many different types of minerals and rocks on display. White quartz, green limestone, and a dark-colored rock called kimberlite were just a few names he read on the display cases. There was even an exhibit of a massive meteorite. It weighed fifteen tons and was ten feet tall. According to at least one dinosaur book Finn had read, a meteorite was responsible for the extinction of the dinosaurs.

Finn let go of the handle and walked over to a display case labeled Gemstones. He leaned against the glass and read the signs.

"These are amazing," Finn said. "Check out these garnets, rubies, and sapphires."

Then something sparkled. It was one of the gems in the display. Finn thought about the truck driver and the sparkling light he had seen.

"You can't afford them, so stop looking," Botts said, grinning.

"And we need to hustle," Bart added. "I can hear the director's voice echoing from the other gallery."

After Bart moved a rope blocking the exit, they walked into the Dinosaur Gallery. As they entered, Finn noticed another donation raptor with a sign around its neck, similar to the one in front of the gift shop.

"These raptors must be everywhere," Finn said, pointing.

"One in each gallery of the museum," Bart responded. "Just a reminder to donate."

"Over here!" a voice shouted. Finn and Botts turned around to see their friend Tess.

She was waving her hands near the T. rex and Triceratops exhibit. Tess had come earlier to save them a place to sleep.

Finn and Botts helped Bart guide the cart over to the new exhibit location. Bart pushed the cart up against a nearby wall.

"Both of you were a great help," Bart said. "Have fun tonight!"

"Thanks, Bart," Finn replied. Finn and Botts picked up their bags and ran to the opposite side of the gallery where Tess was standing.

"I've saved a spot for both of you right here, next to the Triceratops," Tess said proudly.

The exhibit featured a T. rex emerging through two pine trees with his jaws wide open, ready to attack a Triceratops. The Triceratops was ready to lunge forward with its three huge horns.

Botts stared at the exhibit for a minute. "I think you're right, Finn. Triceratops will watch out for us the entire night."

Finn walked over and read the exhibit sign to himself.

> *Tyrannosaurus rex, the tyrant lizard king.*
>
> *T. rex was forty feet long and over fifteen feet tall.*
>
> *With its bone-crunching teeth, it could eat large dinosaurs, including triceratops.*

*So much for getting any protection out of T. tops,* thought Finn. Suddenly, he heard a voice he recognized.

"Students, I want you all over here now," the voice said.

He turned around. It was Director Thornton. She had just entered the gallery, and she did not look happy.

# CHAPTER FOUR

"Our security staff just discovered some students wandering through our other galleries and touching some of the exhibits," Director Thornton said with a frown. "Please stay in *this* gallery. We have alarm sensors and cameras throughout the museum. You don't want the unexpected surprise of confronting a security guard. If a security guard is asked to find you, your parents will be contacted and asked to pick you up tonight."

"Dinah is acting a little like a Dinah-saur," Danny whispered to Manny, who snickered under his breath.

Finn overheard both of them and looked over.

Director Thornton's frown turned to a smile. "I want to welcome all of you to our museum sleepover. Our sleepover benefits the Save the Dinosaurs fundraiser. As you know, this fundraiser will help the museum complete the new dinosaur exhibit in this gallery. We appreciate all of you for coming. Tonight, we'll see several of our galleries. We'll also be doing a dinosaur scavenger hunt. But before we begin, pizza and drinks are available in the Oceans Gallery behind you. Please follow the signs and be back here in forty-five minutes."

Finn, Botts, and Tess walked over to the Oceans Gallery entrance. On the right was a coral reef with sea urchins, a spiny lobster, and a big puffer fish. On the left was a display of bottlenose and spinner dolphins, sea lions, and walruses. And in the center, suspended from the ceiling with two thick cables, was the display of a twenty-foot-long great white shark, its mouth full of several rows of jagged, sharp teeth.

After stacking his plate with pizza slices, Botts walked over to the shark. He stopped and looked closely at its mouth. "Come see these teeth!" Botts shouted to Tess and Finn.

Suddenly, there was a loud thud.

Everyone looked in Botts's direction. Botts had fallen backward onto the floor. Pizza slices had splattered everywhere. The shark's mouth was wide open, its head turned toward Botts. It looked as if it were ready to lunge at the pizza for a snack and then at Botts for the main course.

"Did you see that?" Botts yelled, lying on the ground. "That shark just looked at me and opened its mouth."

The McKinnsey twins witnessed the whole event from where they were standing.

"Even cavemen had more coordination than you," Manny said loudly.

"But it's OK," Danny added, trying hard to appear serious. "Cavemen didn't mind eating things off the ground." He looked over at Botts and yelled, "Hey, caveman, enjoy eating your mess with your pet shark!"

Manny and Danny both burst out laughing.

Finn and Tess raced over to help Botts get up. A door then opened near the northeast corner of the Oceans Gallery. It was Bart. He hurried toward them.

"I'm sorry," Bart said. "Didn't expect you to drop your pizza. Just wanted to have some fun."

"You did that?" Botts questioned. "How?"

Bart motioned to all of them. "Come with me, and I'll show you."

They all followed Bart back to the door in the corner and up a stairway into a room. The room had three computer monitors on a long curved desk. Behind the desk was a huge wall-mounted screen. The screen displayed twenty-four different images.

"Welcome to the security control room," Bart said. "Look at this screen." Bart pointed his finger to one of the screens on the far-right side. "The great white shark is my favorite. Security cameras are in both eyes. When someone walks by, I touch the monitor screen here, and the shark's head turns, or I can open its mouth by touching here. Behind the shark is the giant squid. Both of its eyes have cameras too."

Bart paused. "Check out this screen on the left. It looks like two girls are near the squid's thirty-foot tentacles."

"It's Lulu and Deedee," Tess said.

"Go ahead," Bart insisted. "Try moving one of the squid's eyes by touching this place on the screen."

Tess reached over and aimed the left eye at the two girls. They continued to talk and walk toward the eye.

"Move it again," Finn said. "See if you can get them to notice the eye."

Tess waited and moved the eye again, just as they walked past. The moving eye caught Lulu's attention. She looked at Deedee and pointed.

"Do it again while they're looking," Finn said.

Tess moved the eye a third time. Deedee let out a scream.

They all laughed as they watched Lulu and Deedee run away.

"I better let all of you get back," Bart said. "It looks like Director Thornton is starting to ask students to return to the Dinosaur Gallery."

"Thanks for letting us inside," Finn said. "I guess we now know who really runs this place."

All three of them tromped down the stairs and went out the door. As they walked toward the archway leading back into the Dinosaur Gallery, Finn looked at the great white shark display. The pizza spill had been completely cleaned up.

"There's Botts," one of the staff members called out. "We saved you some pizza after that little fall over there but couldn't find you. We felt pretty confident the shark didn't get you."

The staff member walked over and handed Botts a new plate of pizza slices and a rag to wipe the pizza sauce off his clothes.

"Thanks," Botts said sheepishly.

All twenty-two students were seated on the floor when they walked into the Dinosaur Gallery. Director Thornton was in front, handing Ms. Twitchel a stack of papers. They hurried over and sat down in the back row.

Within minutes, the main overhead lights went out, and the security lights came on. The gallery was covered in dim yellow light, except for small exhibit lights shining directly on the dinosaurs.

Finn gazed at the raptor exhibit nearby. The exhibit lights seemed to make them come alive. How could he ever outrun a raptor? His imagination started to make him feel uneasy. Some students began to scream. Instantly, the director's flashlight went on.

"Are you ready for our dinosaur scavenger hunt?" Director Thornton asked in an excited voice. "Your teacher will give each of you a puzzle to complete," she continued. "The puzzle has fourteen questions on it. Please read the instructions. You'll find the answers you need on the display signs in front of each of the dinosaur exhibits. You can start with any question. When you've finished, please return them to me. You have one hour. Feel free to work in groups. Afterward, we'll meet in the Prehistoric Mammals Gallery, on your left."

The director flashed her light toward the crate that Finn and Botts had helped push. "And those who turn in their puzzle worksheets will be able to make a replica of one of our newest fossils, inside that crate."

"What kind of dinosaur is in there?" Taz asked. Taz was a school friend of Botts's.

"Complete the puzzle, and you'll know the answer," Director Thornton replied.

Ms. Twitchel handed a stack of puzzle worksheets to Finn. He passed them along to

Botts and Tess. Finn looked at the questions. Some of them had words he couldn't even pronounce. And with just the glow of the security lights, the worksheet was a little difficult to see.

Finn looked over at Botts. "How are we going to finish this in one hour?"

# CHAPTER FIVE

"Let's just sit back and relax so I can finish my pizza," Botts suggested, "then get the answers from Louis and Victor."

"Let's keep it simple," Tess said, ignoring Botts. "We'll start with the first question. I think I know the answer, and it's right across from us in the corner."

"I agree," Finn replied. "The sooner we start, the faster we finish. And using Louis and Victor will get us the wrong answers." Finn could see students already beginning to gather around the display signs at the exhibits nearest them.

"Tess, read the first question," Finn said.

*A dinosaur with about seventeen bony plates.*

"Ankylosaurus is over in that display, with the big club at the end of its tail," Tess said, pointing. "But it has knobs and spikes."

Tess pointed toward the Stegosaurus skeleton nearby.

"That's my guess," Tess said. "Let's go check it out."

The Stegosaurus exhibit was next to the Paleontology Lab. A window allowed visitors to peer inside and watch museum staff prepare fossils for display. Tess reached the exhibit first and read the display sign.

Finn walked over to the lab window. The lights were off, and no one was inside. Finn looked at the floor near the lab door.

"Botts," Finn said. "Look at this long trail of gray-colored dirt."

"Why would someone leave a mess like that on the museum floor?" Botts asked.

"Someone must have been in a hurry," Finn replied.

Tess yelled out. "Got this one right! It says seventeen plates right on the sign."

"Nice work," Finn said. "Let's do the raptor question in the middle of the worksheet. No reason to find something else when the raptor exhibit is right in front of us."

Tess read question seven.

*The biggest known dromaeosaur, also known as raptor.*

Finn walked over to get a closer look at the raptor exhibit. It had replicas of ancient ferns and trees scattered throughout the display. Four lifelike models of Velociraptors were on the left side, each in a running pose. On the right were three replicas of a raptor called Deinonychus. They were preying on what looked like an Iguanodon. In the rear was a tall dinosaur skeleton emerging from the trees.

"This should be easy," Botts said. He looked down at the display sign and pointed. "It says right here that Deinonychus was twelve feet tall and Velociraptor was six feet tall. Not hard to guess at this point, right?"

Finn looked down at the worksheet question again. In parentheses, next to question seven, were the words *Taller than twelve feet.*

Finn looked up. "It's not Deinonychus. It's something bigger."

"But there is no other raptor here," Tess said. "The dino skeleton in the back is probably an Allosaurus. It's just too big." Tess looked puzzled.

"But why is it with the raptor exhibit?" asked Finn.

Finn took the worksheet from Tess and raced around the corner to the rear of the exhibit. As he approached the fierce-looking skeleton, he noticed a huge sickle-shaped talon on both hind legs. It was nine inches long. Definitely something to avoid if you're being chased by one. Finn began to read the sign.

> *Likely the biggest raptor that*
> *ever lived, Utahraptor was*
> *about twenty-three feet long and*
> *weighed over half a ton.*

Feeling proud, Finn turned around and walked back to Tess and Botts. As he filled out the worksheet, he glanced over at the exit leading into the Minerals and Gems Gallery. Parked behind some plants was a steel cart with a crate on top.

"Botts!" Finn shouted. "Come see this."

Botts walked toward Finn.

"Look at this crate," Finn continued. "Isn't this the same crate we helped Bart push?" Finn pointed to the numbers and letters on the crate.

"You're right," Botts responded. "Why would someone move the cart from where we left it—to here?"

"I don't know," Finn responded. "But I do know that Director Thornton is going to be mad if she notices the cart was moved again. And I don't want to get blamed. I think we need to find Bart and tell him."

Finn walked over to Tess and handed her the worksheet.

"Utahraptor," Finn said. "No Allosaurus here."

"That's a big raptor!" Tess exclaimed.

"You can thank me later," Finn responded. "The T. rex display has too many people. So let's do the next question, rather than going back to the top. And I'm betting our answer is at the back of the gallery."

Finn pointed at two massive dinosaur skeletons facing each other. One was so tall, museum visitors could walk under its neck. Both towered over all the other exhibits in the gallery. Botts read question eight.

*Which is taller: Brachiosaurus or Argentinosaurus?*

"The one we can walk under is my pick," Botts chuckled.

They made their way through the gallery toward the two towering skeletons. There were students in front of nearly every exhibit in the gallery now. Botts stopped right next to the front right foot of the taller dinosaur and gazed up. It was so tall that its skull almost touched the gallery ceiling. Finn stopped in front of the exhibit and stared at both of the enormous skeletons. Tess kept walking until she reached the display sign on the other side.

Finn didn't notice Manny and Danny watching them.

"Look!" Manny shouted, pointing at Finn and Botts. "There are the cavemen."

Finn turned around.

"At least some of us will be getting a cast of a new dinosaur fossil when we turn in our puzzles," Finn said, fuming.

They both ignored Finn's response. Neither of them had their puzzle worksheets.

"Finn, tell Botts to be careful," Danny said. "Although Botts is slightly smarter than that dinosaur, I don't want him to forget where he's standing. He might get stomped on."

"We'll be hanging out with the raptors—the smart dinosaurs—if you need some help," Manny added as they walked away, laughing.

Botts hadn't noticed them. He was still gazing up at Argentinosaurus.

"Listen!" Tess shouted. "I've got the answer to question eight. As tall as a six-story building and three school buses long, Argentinosaurus is one of the biggest known dinosaurs. At seventy feet high and over one hundred feet long, this sauropod towered over the forty-foot Brachiosaurus. Three questions down, eleven to go."

Finn wasn't listening. He was following the twins with his eyes as they wandered toward the exit that led into the Minerals and Gems Gallery. When they reached the plants next to the raptor exhibit, they looked both ways. Suddenly both twins ducked under the rope and disappeared into the lowly lit gallery.

*What are Manny and Danny doing?* thought Finn. He glanced over again. He thought something was wrong. The steel cart with the crate they had pushed earlier was missing. Finn turned and hurried over to Botts and Tess.

"The crate with the new dinosaur fossils is gone," Finn said with alarm. "Someone took it while we were standing right here."

"Maybe someone pushed it back over near the new exhibit, where you and Bart left it," Tess suggested.

They all looked over at the new exhibit and nearby lab. They could see nothing. Finn then scanned the entire gallery. No crate.

"The McKinnsey twins just sneaked out of the gallery," Finn said. "And now the crate with the new dino fossils is gone. I'm going to see if Bart is in the control room. He can track them down by using the security cameras. I'll be back in a minute."

Finn walked toward the Oceans Gallery entrance. He looked to see that no one was watching and quietly slipped inside.

After sprinting past the dolphin and seal exhibits, Finn reached the door leading to the security control room.

He turned the knob. It was locked.

He knocked. No answer.

Finn dashed back into the Dinosaur Gallery and looked over at the exit where Manny and Danny had left. Director Thornton was with a group of students immediately next to the exit. They were talking about the Elasmosaurus in front of them. He saw Tess and Botts standing in front of the Parasaurolophus in the middle of the gallery and ran toward them.

"Just in time," Tess said. She read question four.

*A dinosaur with a large hollow crest of bone on its head.*

"Let me introduce you to Parasaurolophus," Tess continued. "The dinosaur that could use its crest to make loud trumpet-like sounds."

"I think I've heard those kinds of sounds before," Finn said, smiling. "Those are the sounds Botts makes when he sleeps."

"You just wish you could sleep like me," Botts said, smiling back. "Like a rock and with no crazy dreams—"

"Listen," Finn interrupted. "The security control room was locked, and there was no sign of Bart. So here's my plan." He leaned over to both of them and whispered, "Tess, you distract the director and the other students while Botts and I sneak into the Minerals and Gems Gallery. We will go to the warehouse to get the caveman costumes."

"You mean we're going to *put on* the caveman costumes?" Botts asked.

"Yes," Finn said in an urgent voice. "If we can find the twins, the caveman costumes will hopefully scare them into returning to the Dinosaur Gallery with the rest of the class. Not only will we prevent them from doing something that embarrasses the whole class, but if the twins took the cart, we'll also return the crate and make the museum director happy."

"Well, it's time to show the twins that cavemen aren't as dumb as they think," Botts asserted.

"But I'm really hoping we can find Bart first," replied Finn. "I'm betting he'll be able to help us find the twins and the crate much faster."

"But you both know this could get you into trouble, just like the twins," Tess warned.

"That's the chance we take," replied Finn.

"At least we're trying to help," said Botts.

While Finn and Botts moved toward the exit into the Minerals and Gems Gallery, Tess joined the student group listening to Director Thornton.

"It was forty-six feet long and had an extremely long neck, with four flippers for limbs," Director Thornton explained. "In fact, Elasmosaurus was one of the biggest known plesiosaurs ever identified."

Tess had to act before the director or the students noticed Finn and Botts trying to sneak away. She thrust her hand in the air and said the first thing that came to her mind. "Director Thornton, do you think dinosaurs barfed when they got sick?"

All eyes instantly shifted to Tess. Director Thornton was now staring at the ground in thought. It had worked. Botts and Finn slipped under the rope and ran into the gallery.

As Tess watched Finn and Botts leave, Director Thornton looked up. Tess quickly jerked her head back toward the director.

"I'm sure they did," Director Thornton replied.

"I bet they farted too," said a kid named Max.

Everyone started laughing.

"Quiet, please," the director interrupted, with an annoyed look on her face. "For those who are interested, let's move to the Therizinosaurus behind you. We only have twenty minutes left to complete our puzzles."

The question had worked. Tess stared into the Minerals and Gems Gallery. She wondered whether Finn's idea to find Bart and the McKinnsey twins was really worth it. Finn and Botts might be sent home if they got caught.

# CHAPTER SIX

Finn and Botts walked past the meteorite exhibit in the middle of the Minerals and Gems Gallery. Finn noticed it first. Another trail of grayish dirt on the ground. Just like in the Dinosaur Gallery. But this time, there were some small rocks mixed in with the dirt. And these rocks sparkled.

"Who do you think is doing this?" Botts asked, pointing to the trail of dirt. He looked up at Finn.

"I don't know," Finn replied. "But if we find the twins or Bart, maybe we'll have an answer."

After hiding behind Spinosaurus in the rotunda while the janitor walked into another gallery, Finn and Botts entered the double doors of the warehouse.

"There they are," Botts said, pointing to the caveman costumes.

"And look what's gone," Finn sputtered with alarm. He pointed to some nearby empty hooks. "The raptor costumes are missing." Finn looked around the warehouse to see if they had been moved. They were nowhere.

"Manny and Danny must have taken them," Botts said. "Who else would have done it?"

Finn walked past Botts, then reached up and pulled the first caveman costume and mask off the wall hook. But they were both too large.

Finn handed the costume to Botts. "This is for you."

Botts put on the costume and pulled the mask over his face. As Finn put on the other caveman costume, Botts looked around the warehouse through the eye slits in his mask. He noticed a replica of a wooden club leaning against the wall where his costume had been hanging.

"Every caveman needs a club," Botts chuckled. He walked over and grabbed the club.

"I'm ready," Finn said. "Let's get out of here before someone finds us."

Finn's mask had shoulder-length black hair. And Botts's mask had scruffy, frazzled brown hair. Their costumes made them look like they were wearing real animal skins.

As they walked back toward the warehouse doors, Finn picked up a spear with a metal tip lying on one of the tables. "At least one of us has a real weapon," Finn said with a quiet laugh.

Finn reached the warehouse doors first and peered out into the rotunda. There was no one around except Spinosaurus and the donation raptor near the gift shop. One dead dinosaur and one replica. Nothing he or Botts needed to worry about.

Finn quickly walked over to the floor-plan sign near the ticket counter. He pointed at the Ancient Civilizations Gallery. "Let's start with this one and see if we can find Bart or the twins. It's in the middle and leads back to the Dinosaur Gallery. None of the students should be walking around in there, so none of them will see us."

"I'm ready to find those wannabe raptors," Botts said.

They ran out of the rotunda and into the Ancient Civilizations Gallery. Unique clothing from early civilizations was on display on the right and left sides of the gallery. Some of the clothing included Roman togas, Egyptian kilts, and Chinese silk robes. Finn could hear the faint voices of the students in the other gallery. But there was no sign of Bart or the McKinnsey twins.

When they reached the entrance to the Dinosaur Gallery, Finn scanned the exhibits around them to make sure no students were looking in their direction.

He glanced over at Gallimimus. It was right next to the entrance near the Elasmosaurus. He recalled reading about it in the dinosaur encyclopedia. It was built like an ostrich and three times as tall as a human. He wished he and Botts could just jump on and use Gallimimus to run around the museum until they spotted Bart or the twins. With the ability to reach speeds of up to fifty miles per hour, Gallimimus was one of the fastest dinosaurs and could probably cover the entire museum in minutes. They ran

65

quietly into the Prehistoric Mammals Gallery on the right. Finn peered around the corner. He could now hear Director Thornton's voice.

"You've seen some of the dinosaurs that lived in different parts of the world," the director said. "Now let's look at some prehistoric mammals and early humans. We'll first start with early humans, popularly referred to as cavemen and cavewomen."

The director came into view. Finn watched her walk around the T. rex and Triceratops display and move toward them. A group of students trailed behind her. Finn's heart started beating faster. There was not enough time to run out of the gallery without being seen.

"Nowhere to go—except in here," Finn said, pointing. "The cavemen display. They'll never recognize us in there."

Finn and Botts climbed over the handrail. A number of cavemen and cavewomen models

were in the display in various poses. But none were near the realistic-looking cave on the left side. They found a place to stand near the cave opening. A simulated fire using a fan, fabric, and colored lights was in front. A small fake animal was cooking over the flames.

"You've got to make yourself look real," Finn said in a low voice. "You can't just stand up, leaning against the cave wall. Crouch down near the fire. Act like you're hungry. That should be easy for you."

Finn decided to hold up his spear as if he were going to throw it. He turned away from Botts and faced the other gallery exhibits. Throwing a spear at nothing didn't make much sense to Finn, but he couldn't think of anything else to do.

The class entered the gallery and surrounded Director Thornton in front of the exhibit.

The director began. "Cavemen and cave-women lived during the last ice age. Caves have been found with crude animal paintings similar to the ones you see near the cave entrance."

Finn was trying his best to stay still, but the spear was becoming heavy. He hoped Botts was not moving.

"What's the caveman doing with the spear?" a girl named Veronica asked.

Director Thornton looked over and gazed silently for a moment. "I guess he's protecting the group from an intruder. I don't remember seeing this caveman before. This must be a new model. I'll ask the staff about him."

Taz waved his hand wildly.

"You also may want to ask the staff about the wild-haired caveman crouched near the fire," he said, grinning. "His hands are cooking in the fire. Soon the rest of the group will be eating him rather than what's on the spit."

The entire class laughed. Finn grumbled silently to himself but remained motionless. He did not want to be detected.

"You're right," Director Thornton responded. "I'll make sure that particular caveman is moved. Let's continue down the gallery and visit the giant ground sloth."

As soon as the class had reached the other exhibit, Finn turned toward Botts.

"Cavemen don't put their hands in fire," Finn whispered. "In fact, no one puts their hands in fire. What were you thinking?"

"I just wanted to see how it felt," Botts replied. "Especially the little fan—"

Finn raised his hand to quiet Botts. He could hear the sound of faint voices.

"Did you hear that?" Finn whispered.

The voices started again.

Botts nodded.

They both turned around. The voices were not coming from the students or anyone else in the gallery. The voices were coming from inside the cave.

# CHAPTER SEVEN

Finn pulled off his mask and crept toward the cave opening. He peered inside. The cave was dark. He turned on the small flashlight his dad had given him. The voices were coming from the very back of the cave. He shined the flashlight along the plywood floor until the light reached a square object.

"I see some kind of opening in the very back," Finn said. "It has a cover on it. Let's go see what it is."

Finn laid his spear down and walked into the cave. After pulling off his mask, Botts followed.

Finn reached the opening in the rear and looked down.

"It's covered by a steel grate," Finn said. "I can see a ladder underneath that goes down to a tunnel. It sounds like the voices are coming from somewhere inside the tunnel."

"What do you think this is?" Botts asked.

"This must be a vent," Finn replied. "But I doubt Manny and Danny are down there."

"And look at the dirt scattered around the grate," Botts said, pointing.

"It looks like the same gray dirt we saw on the floor in the museum," Finn added. "Maybe we can figure out where the dirt is coming from if we climb down and look around."

After Botts laid his club down, he and Finn grabbed the rectangular grate and lifted. The grate came up with almost no noise. They carefully set it down on the floor next to the opening and peered down. The metal ladder descended at least ten feet before it reached the tunnel.

Finn went down first. Botts followed.

Finn reached the bottom step and jumped to the tunnel floor. It was covered with gravel—and gray dirt. He picked up the dirt and examined it.

"So here's where the dirt is coming from," Finn whispered, looking around the tunnel.

Finn saw cart tracks leading in both directions in the low light. The light came from light bulbs strung together along the left side of the tunnel wall. The air in the tunnel had a musty smell.

"Who would dig a tunnel under a museum?" Botts asked.

"Let's go find out," Finn replied. "The voices are coming from this direction." He pointed north.

Finn and Botts walked slowly through the tunnel in the direction of the noises. Finn felt a cold sweat on his face. There was nowhere to hide if they saw someone.

They finally came to a large opening in a concrete wall. The opening was covered by a metal screen.

"It feels like we've walked from one side of the mammals gallery to the other," Finn said in a low voice.

Finn and Botts peered through the metal screen together. Beyond the screen, they saw a room filled with steel containers, machines, and tables.

Each of the containers was marked Antwerp Gem Co. Some of them were open. Inside were gray and black rocks of different shapes and sizes. And all of them sparkled. Just like the sparkle Finn saw in the truck in the rear parking lot of the museum.

Between two of the machines was a table with a crate on top. Near the table was a tall, thin worker. His narrow face seemed to push his lips down, giving him a permanent frown. He was packing the sparkling rocks from the containers into the crate, while a big older worker with a mustache carried the empty steel containers back to the shelves.

"Nothing but pretty rocks for this shipment," the skinny worker said with a sinister look on his face. "I think we should all get a few of them for workin' so hard." He held one up to the light. "Look at how those rough diamonds glitter in these rocks. Just waitin' for someone to take them out. Probably wouldn't hurt to take a few of these rough sapphires either."

"We'll get paid when we're finished," the older worker responded. "Just make sure they all get into the crate. We don't want to lose one. Thornton won't think twice about what's in there as long as it feels like it's full of bones."

"They're stealing diamonds," Finn gasped. He couldn't believe what he was watching.

"We need to tell someone," Botts muttered.

"First, we need to get out of here—alive," Finn said, gulping. His voice was trembling. Suddenly there was a loud noise, and the screen started to open.

"Remember to keep the noise down," the thin one said. "This shipment needs to be loaded tonight without anyone asking questions. Even though the boss is watching with the cameras, we still need to be careful. That school sleepover is going on tonight."

"We've got to make it down the tunnel before they see us," Finn whispered. "No time to try climbing back up the vent. Go!"

Botts had already started running. As Finn looked back, the screen was completely open, and the big worker was pushing the cart into the tunnel.

Finn and Botts raced passed the vent that led back up to the cave. Within seconds, they had run past another vent shaft.

"Where are we going?" Botts said, trying to catch his breath.

They could hear the cart's wheels.

"I don't know—just anywhere they won't find us," Finn said. "Keep moving!"

The tunnel sloped upward. At the top of the slope, Finn and Botts both saw a steel door. Finn ran past Botts and reached the door first. Finn looked down.

"This door has no handle!" Finn exclaimed.

The sound of the cart's wheels grew louder.

"But there has to be a way out," Finn said. A look of panic crossed his face.

Botts moved past Finn and leaned against the door with all his weight. His eyes bulged slightly as he pushed and grunted. He stopped and gasped.

"That grunting sounded so natural," Finn teased. "Maybe you're a caveman on the inside as well."

Botts panted. "This door is not moving anywhere. Maybe the door opens automatically."

"That's it," Finn said. "Botts, sometimes you're useful. Start looking for something that opens the door."

Finn looked on the left side of the tunnel while Botts looked on the right.

"Nothing on my side," Finn said.

"I don't see anything except this lever," Botts said.

"Try pushing on it!" Finn replied in a frantic voice.

"But what if the door makes a sound when it opens?" Botts questioned.

"No choice," Finn replied. "If we stay here, we'll be caught. Push it!"

Botts pushed. Nothing.

He pulled. The lever moved downward. The steel door made a creaking sound and opened.

"Move!" Finn said.

Finn and Botts entered a dark room. The steel door closed behind them. Finn peered through a window and saw some of the students in his class near the Stegosaurus.

"This must be the Paleontology Lab," Finn said. "We're back in the museum."

Museum crates and carts were in the back of the lab. Tables in the middle of the lab were covered with dusty brushes, scalpels, bowls, and a few bones encased in plaster. A microscope, chisel, and hammer were on a workbench in the front.

"Why would they haul rocks through a tunnel and into this lab?" Botts asked.

"This must be a cover for their operation," Finn explained. "They use the crates to sneak the raw diamonds and gems out of the building and into the truck. That way no one in the museum suspects anything is wrong. The crate we just saw in the tunnel even had a real dinosaur bone on top of the rocks, just in case someone looked inside. We really need to find Bart."

*Creeeeeeeeeak!* The steel door began to open.

# CHAPTER EIGHT

Finn and Botts dashed around the tables and headed for the door at the other side of the room. The door led into the Minerals and Gems Gallery. They could hear the big worker yelling to himself just behind the steel door. The cart was stuck.

Botts grabbed a hammer and chisel from the workbench as he ran. *Not exactly a club and spear,* thought Botts. *But they might be good for defending ourselves if confronted by diamond thieves.*

Finn turned his head around to see what Botts was doing.

"No such thing as cavemen without weapons," Botts muttered as he showed Finn the hammer and chisel.

"That big guy probably eats hammers and chisels for lunch," Finn said, frustrated. "Hustle!"

They hurried out the lab door toward a display of clear-colored rocks.

Student voices echoed from the other galleries.

"Look," Botts whispered.

Finn and Botts both stopped.

In the middle of the gallery were two raptors. But they were not donation raptors. They were pushing a cart with a crate on it toward the front entrance of the museum.

Finn could feel tingling throughout his body. He knew they had to do something quickly. The big worker with the other cart could be coming out the lab door any minute.

"It must be the twins in the raptor costumes," Finn said in a quiet voice. "We finally caught up with them. I can't believe they're part of this." Finn turned toward Botts. "I think it's time to catch a couple of raptors."

"I've been waiting for this moment!" Botts exclaimed.

Finn and Botts pulled on their masks and crept toward them.

Botts's shoes squeaked along the floor. The raptor closest to them startled at the noise and turned around, with the beam of its flashlight now centered on Botts.

"What's your worry?" Botts asked. "Just two dumb cavemen trying to stop you."

The raptors turned and ran with the cart as fast as they could toward the gallery exit. And Finn and Botts were right behind them.

· · ·

Tess, Director Thornton, and the rest of the students heard the voices and rumble of the cart in the Minerals and Gems Gallery. Director Thornton looked worried. She pushed a button on her phone.

"Bart, are you there?" she asked.

The other end of the phone line was only silence. She tried again with no response.

Then Director Thornton pushed another button. "Change of plans," she said, trying to act calm. "Rather than going back to the Dinosaur Gallery, we'll walk straight through this gallery to the rotunda. I'll introduce you to my favorite dinosaur. Let's go now."

*Something is wrong,* thought Tess. She wondered if Finn and Botts had been caught.

# CHAPTER NINE

Finn was surprised at how fast the raptors were running while pushing the cart. He was surprised they were running at all. Were they really scared of their caveman costumes?

Finn glanced back over his shoulder. Botts was struggling to keep up with him. Finn turned back to watch the raptors push the cart through the gallery exit.

Suddenly, there was a thud and a groan. Finn peered through the slits in his mask. Botts had run into the meteorite exhibit and fallen over. Finn turned around and ran back to help him.

"This meteorite is going to make more than just the dinosaurs extinct if you're not careful," Finn said.

"These masks are almost impossible to see and breathe out of," Botts said, gasping for air.

"We can't take the masks off yet," Finn said. "I don't want our raptors to know who we are."

After Finn helped Botts stand up, they ran toward the gallery exit. When they reached the entrance to the rotunda, they both stopped. Finn quickly scanned the entire area. No sign of the raptors anywhere.

"How could they have gotten away?" Finn asked.

Botts pointed.

The two raptors were standing still right next to the donation raptor. Their claws were upright, and their jaws were open, just like the donation raptor. The raptors had hidden the cart behind a reception desk where one of the security guards had been standing earlier. He and Botts walked toward them.

"Did you really expect us to believe you two—dressed up as raptors—were just some more donation dinos?" blurted Botts.

Suddenly, Finn and Botts heard the clear sound of voices. Director Thornton, Ms. Twitchel, and the rest of the class were walking toward the rotunda.

Finn leaned over to Botts and whispered, "The director will send us home if she finds out we left the group and took these costumes. But if we trap the twins with their raptor costumes on and explain to her that they were helping the diamond thieves move these carts, maybe we have a chance of staying. Follow me."

Finn ran quickly behind one of the motionless raptors. Botts handed the chisel to Finn

and got behind the other raptor just as Director Thornton walked into the rotunda with the rest of the students.

She cautiously looked around, staring at the warehouse doors, then over to the main entrance and the gift shop, then back.

"I want everyone near the dinosaur in the middle," Director Thornton requested.

Tess and the rest of the class walked toward the gigantic skeleton on display.

Director Thornton began. "This is our Spinosaurus. Spinosaurus means *spine lizard*. This dinosaur roamed the swamps of North Africa ninety-five million years ago. The long, thin bones jutting from its back supported a skin membrane that, together, formed a sail. The sail could have been used to regulate body temperature or attract mates."

"Excuse me," Deedee interrupted. "Is there a reason why you now have two more donation raptors?" She pointed toward the gift shop.

"As well as two cavemen," Veronica added in an alarmed voice. "That one over there with the frazzled hair looks just like the one we saw in the cavemen exhibit."

Tess smiled. Crouched behind each of the new raptors was a caveman. One caveman was holding a hammer upright over one raptor, and the other caveman was pointing a chisel at the other raptor. It could only be Finn and Botts.

The director walked over and looked carefully. "Things are getting very strange around here," she said. "These models were not here when we closed today."

Taz was already standing near the new raptors after reading the donation sign on the first raptor. "Let's see how hungry this one is in the middle," Taz joked.

Taz dumped a pocketful of coins into the raptor's mouth. Immediately it began to cough, and the coins came spewing out of its mouth. Without warning, both raptors turned and shoved Finn and Botts to the ground. They ran to the cart behind the security desk and pushed it toward the warehouse doors.

Finn stood up quickly and watched the raptors run toward the warehouse doors. Did Manny and Danny think they could escape?

Suddenly an ear-piercing roar came from inside the warehouse.

The students screamed as Finn watched in horror.

# CHAPTER TEN

As the two raptors reached the warehouse entrance, a Tyrannosaurus rex crashed through the warehouse doors. Its jaws gaped wide, and its head moved back and forth. Sharp claws swiped the air.

Students raced back into the galleries. Director Thornton yelled for everyone to remain calm. Finn stared through the slits in his mask in amazement.

"This is the remote-controlled robot Bart was talking about!" Finn exclaimed.

"Who's controlling it?" Botts asked.

Both Finn and Botts watched as the two raptors tried to turn the cart to avoid running into the T. rex. But the cart was moving too fast and tipped over, causing the crate to crash onto its side. Diamond-covered rocks and dinosaur bones tumbled onto the museum floor. The two raptors reached down and grabbed as many rocks as they could, then sprinted for the warehouse doors.

"Hands up and don't move!" someone shouted.

Suddenly everyone stopped and looked toward the main entrance of the museum.

Police officers came rushing through the doors. Guns were pointed at both the raptors and the cavemen. The T. rex immediately stopped moving.

An officer in a long dark overcoat stepped forward. "Remove your masks."

Finn and Botts pulled off their masks. The raptors followed.

Finn looked over in shock. The two people in the raptor costumes were not Manny and Danny. They were the two security guards they had seen in the rotunda on their way to the Dinosaur Gallery earlier in the evening.

Director Thornton walked over to the man with the dark overcoat and whispered to him. She pointed to Finn and Botts as she talked. After she had finished talking, the man walked over to them.

"Congratulations," the man with the over-coat said. "I'm Detective Worthington. We've been trying to catch these thieves for years. We suspect they're part of a well-organized diamond-theft operation. We didn't know who was doing it or how it was being done until tonight. Director Thornton called last night about dinosaur bones missing. When she called again tonight about a crate being moved, seeing extra cavemen models in an exhibit, and strange noises, we knew something was up. We appreciate your help. It's not very often a pair of cavemen outsmart a couple of raptors."

The two security guards in raptor costumes were now being led away by police officers. Finn and Botts watched as Detective Worthington walked over to the crate and carefully looked at the contents.

"As you can see, our raptors were interested in more than just bones," the detective said. "Looks like more diamonds and other gems."

"And we can show you the tunnel leading to the location where they were filling the crates," Finn offered. "You should send some of your officers into the tunnel right now. We saw two of the thieves down there. Both were loading

diamonds into crates. You can get to the tunnel through the door inside the Paleontology Lab."

Detective Worthington immediately looked away and shouted to two of his officers to come over. Finn listened to the detective quickly explain to the officers the use of the tunnel and the location of the lab. The officers nodded and ran straight for the entrance to the Minerals and Gems Gallery.

Detective Worthington turned to face Finn and Botts. "Thank you for your help tonight," "I would like to talk to both of you sometime tomorrow as part of our investigation."

Within minutes, Bart entered the rotunda, escorted by two police officers. He was handcuffed, and his head was down.

Finn was speechless. Finn turned to Detective Worthington.

"Why are you arresting him?" asked Finn, pointing to Bart.

"We knew those cameras allowed him to see nearly everything going on inside the museum," Detective Worthington explained. "But when nothing suspicious was reported, there was little we could do. Until tonight. We believe Bart has been in charge of the whole operation."

Finn couldn't believe what he was hearing. Bart was the one they were trying to warn about the missing crate, yet he knew what was going on the whole time.

"Look what we found!" shouted another officer.

Finn and Botts looked in the direction of the warehouse. Manny and Danny were walking out of the employee break room near the warehouse doors, accompanied by the officer.

"These two were eating candy and watching movies," said the officer. "Something tells me they were in the wrong place."

"You're correct," Director Thornton responded. She had a disappointed look on her face.

Ms. Twitchel took both of the McKinnsey boys back to the gallery to get their bags. Finn guessed their sleepover at the museum had just ended and their parents would be picking them up tonight.

Finn and Botts finished removing their costumes with the help of the museum staff and rejoined the class. Detective Worthington and the rest of the police officers roped off the area where the crate had fallen.

Director Thornton, scowling, pointed to Finn and Botts and asked them to come forward. "Both of you left the group without permission and took costumes that did not belong to you. You also put yourself at risk. However, your actions have helped catch these thieves and prevented valuable museum fossils from being taken. The museum thanks you immensely for your help and courage."

The class cheered.

"It has been quite a night," Director Thornton continued, now smiling. "All of you, back to the Dinosaur Gallery. You've got thirty minutes to be in your sleeping bags." She then looked at Finn and Botts. "You two, wait here."

Director Thornton walked toward the ticket counter in front of the Spinosaurus. She pulled out her phone and made a call. Finn and Botts watched her in silence as she talked. After a few minutes, she returned.

"I'm guessing neither of you finished the puzzle," she said.

Finn and Botts both nodded.

"I've asked the curator to personally help you complete it. He and I both appreciate what you've done tonight. Both of you deserve to take home a cast of our new dinosaur. Be ready at seven o'clock tomorrow morning. Sleep well. You two cavemen deserve it."

# CHAPTER ELEVEN

The next morning, Mr. Fasser arrived at the museum to pick up Finn and Botts. Finn held up a replica of a large talon for his dad to see.

"You two are celebrities!" Mr. Fasser exclaimed. "Here's the lead story in the newspaper."

Finn and Botts read the headline.

**Students Help Catch Diamond Thieves
at Kealstal City Museum!
New Dinosaur Fossils Saved**

"I guess we surprised ourselves," Finn said. "I don't think we expected to save dinosaur fossils."

"And the biggest surprise," Botts added, "was that the dinosaur we saved wasn't really a dinosaur after all."

Mr. Fasser turned toward each of them with a look of surprise. He took the talon from Finn's hand and looked at it carefully.

"You mean *this* does not come from some large, hungry carnivorous dinosaur?" he asked.

"Not even close," Finn replied. "It's as tall as a giraffe but only one-third as heavy."

"So, celebrities," Mr. Fasser said. "What is this new creature?"

"I think you should give him the puzzle," Botts suggested. "Let's see if he can do it."

When they arrived back at Finn's house, Finn handed him a puzzle worksheet.

"There is one letter in each of the fourteen answers that is shaded," Finn explained. "After you answer the rest of the questions, arrange the shaded letters in the correct order at the bottom of the page to find out its name. Botts filled in a few of them for you. Good luck!"

# KEALSTAL CITY MUSEUM
## Puzzle Worksheet

For each clue given, write the name of the dinosaur in the box provided on the right. Then take the letter from each shaded box to form the name of our newest fossil in the boxes provided at the bottom. Have fun!

1. A DINOSAUR WITH ABOUT 17 BONY PLATES (VERY SMALL BRAIN)

`S T E G O S A U R U S`

2. WHICH WAS BIGGER: SPINOSAURUS OR TYRANNOSAURUS REX?

3. ONE OF THE BIGGEST KNOWN LONG-NECKED PLESIOSAURS (ABOUT 46 FEET LONG WITH 4 LARGE FLIPPERS)

4. A DINOSAUR WITH A LARGE HOLLOW CREST OF BONE ON ITS HEAD (POSSIBLY USED TO MAKE SOUNDS TO COMMUNICATE)

`P A R A S A U R O L O P H U S`

5. ONE OF THE LARGEST KNOWN ICHTHYOSAURS (A CROSS BETWEEN A WHALE AND A DOLPHIN AND UP TO 70 FEET LONG)

6. A DINOSAUR WITH 3 ENORMOUS CLAWS ON EACH HAND (PARTLY FEATHERED AND ABOUT 33 FEET LONG)

7. THE BIGGEST KNOWN DROMAEOSAUR, ALSO KNOWN AS A RAPTOR (TALLER THAN 12 FEET)

`U T A H R A P T O R`

8. WHICH IS TALLER: BRACHIOSAURUS OR ARGENTINOSAURUS?

`A R G E N T I N O S A U R U S`

9. A SMALLER TYRANNOSAUR WITH A LONG SNOUT (NICKNAMED "PINOCCHIO REX")

10. ONE OF THE SMALLEST KNOWN DINOSAURS (ABOUT THE SIZE OF A CHICKEN)

11. ONE OF THE FASTEST KNOWN DINOSAURS (BUILT LIKE AN OSTRICH AND UP TO 3 TIMES AS TALL AS A HUMAN. IT HAD THE ABILITY TO RUN AT SPEEDS OF UP TO 50 MPH.)

12. A DINOSAUR WITH 4 TO 6 SPIKES ON ITS FRILL AND 3 HORNS ON ITS HEAD (COUSIN OF TRICERATOPS)

13. THE BIGGEST KNOWN HADROSAUR (DUCK-BILLED DINOSAUR, ABOUT 50 FEET LONG)

14. A DINOSAUR WITH A NEARLY 6-FOOT-LONG NARROW SKULL, UP TO 40 FEET LONG, WITH 132 TEETH (KNOWN AS THE "SUPERCROC")

| U | | | | | | O | A | L | | |
|---|---|---|---|---|---|---|---|---|---|---|
| 9 | 7 | 3 | 13 | 6 | 12 | 11 | 14 | 1 | 8 | 10 | 4 | 5 | 2 |

# ABOUT THE AUTHOR

Stew Knight is the author of the Finn & Botts chapter book series. Despite being one of the most avid readers and attentive students in his second-grade class, he would still find it funny to yell at random moments to disrupt his teacher if she was being too boring—a stunt that his teacher didn't let slide without discipline. But the discipline worked, because Knight's imagination developed to the point where nothing was ever boring again. He thanks his second-grade teacher for helping his imagination grow enough to become an author.

Knight lives in Salt Lake City, Utah, with his wife and very anxious poodle. He enjoys the outdoors and can be found on the ski slopes in the winter, hiking the Wasatch Range of the Rocky Mountains in the spring and summer, and hanging out with the pigs at the annual state fair in the fall.

CPSIA information can be obtained
at www.ICGtesting.com
Printed in the USA
LVHW091022201219
641227LV00002B/265/P